Adaptation: Jane Brierley
Illustrations: Irina Georgeta Pusztai
Graphic design: Zapp

# FAMOUS *Fables* TREASURY

# 1

TORMONT

# THE ANT AND
# THE GRASSHOPPER

Once upon a time, a Grasshopper played all summer long, singing his song and never thinking of the future. Even when autumn came and the leaves turned red and gold, he skipped merrily along the country lanes.

Then the North Wind began to blow. The snow fell, and soon there wasn't a single leaf to nibble. At last the starving Grasshopper knocked on the Ant's door.

"Can you give me some food?" he asked.

"What did you do all summer?" said the Ant, who had worked hard to fill her larder.

"I sang," replied the Grasshopper.

"You sang?" said the Ant, handing him a broom. "Well, now you'll work for your supper!"

# THE FOX AND THE CROW

One day, a Crow was sitting in a tree, holding a bit of cheese in his beak. A Fox walked by just then. The smell of the cheese made his mouth water.

"Why, Master Crow, how pretty you look!" said the sly Fox. "If your voice is as fine as your feathers, you must be the grandest bird in all these woods!"

Now the Crow was an ugly bird, with untidy feathers and a harsh voice. The Fox's praise thrilled him. He opened his beak to sing, and the cheese fell out.

"Ha, ha!" laughed the Fox, snapping up the cheese. "That will teach you not to believe everything you hear!"

# THE FROG AND THE OX

A Frog once sat on a lily pad looking at a large Ox. She said to herself, "Now that's a good size to be!"

The Frog, who was no bigger than your hand, began puffing herself up.

"Look at me!" she cried to the Ox. "Am I as big as you?"

"No," said the Ox.

"Now?" cried the Frog, puffing away.

The Ox just blinked lazily.

"Now?" she said, huffing and puffing,
determined to be bigger than Nature
had meant her to be.

The Ox shook his head. The silly Frog
gave one more puff and . . . she burst!

# THE WOLF AND THE DOG

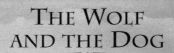

A poor Wolf lived in a nobleman's forest. It was kept just for hunting, and the nobleman's dogs protected it so well that the Wolf could never catch anything. In fact, he was almost nothing but skin and bones!

One day, the Wolf saw a handsome, well-fed Dog strolling through the forest. The Wolf felt too weak to attack. Instead, he went up to the Dog and said politely, "How well-fed you are!"

"Oh, you could be just as well-fed as I am," replied the Dog.

"How?" asked the Wolf eagerly.

"Chase away poachers and beggars, and please the Master and his family," said the Dog. "In return, they'll pet you and feed you well."

The Wolf almost cried for joy, and he immediately set off with the Dog.

As they walked along, he noticed
a worn spot on the Dog's neck.

"What's that?" asked the Wolf.

"Oh, it's just from being tied up."

"Tied up!" gasped the Wolf.

"But not always," said the Dog.

"Thanks anyway," said the Wolf,
turning to go. "My freedom is too high
a price to pay for all your good things."

# THE CITY MOUSE
## AND THE COUNTRY MOUSE

Once upon a time a City Mouse,
who lived in a big house, invited his
country cousin to dinner. He
prepared a delicious feast with food
taken from the grand dining room,
and the two of them sat down to eat.

Suddenly they heard the sound of
scratching on the door of the City
Mouse's hole. A Cat! The City
Mouse took to his heels, and the
Country Mouse scampered after him
as fast as his little feet would go.

When the noise
stopped, the two
cousins came back.
"Now we can finish
our feast," said the City
Mouse, looking very
pleased.

"No thanks!" panted the Country Mouse, quite out of breath from all that running. "Tomorrow you must come and dine with me. I may not have such fine food as you, but at least we won't be afraid of being attacked!"

# THE WOLF
# AND THE LAMB

Someone who wants to do wrong can always find a reason.

A hungry Wolf met a Lamb drinking from a woodland stream.

"How dare you drink from my stream?" growled the Wolf.

"Please don't be angry," said the timid Lamb. "I'm drinking downstream from you, so I can't be doing any harm."

"All the same, you have no business here," said the Wolf. "Anyway, I hear that you told nasty lies about me last year."

"How could that be?" replied the Lamb. "I wasn't even born then."

"Well, your shepherd's dogs are always after me, and I'll have my revenge one way or another," snapped the Wolf. With that, he leaped toward the innocent Lamb who had to run for her life.